Tundra Books, an imprint of Penguin Random House Canada Young Readers, a division of
Penguin Random House of Canada Limited

Library and Archives Canada Cataloguing in Publication

Title: Too many pigs and one big bad wolf / Davide Cali ; illustrated by Marianna Balducci.
Names: Calì, Davide, 1972– author. | Balducci, Marianna, illustrator.
Identifiers: Canadiana (print) 20210182059 | Canadiana (ebook) 20210182067 | ISBN 9780735269910
   (hardcover) | ISBN 9780735269927 (EPUB)
Classification: LCC PZ7.C1283 Too 2022 | DDC j823/.92—dc23

Published simultaneously in the United States of America by Tundra Books of Northern New York,
an imprint of Penguin Random House Canada Young Readers, a division of
Penguin Random House of Canada Limited

Library of Congress Control Number: 2021941646

Edited by Samantha Swenson
Designed by Kelly Hill
The artwork in this book was rendered with illustrations, photographs and a very brave abacus.
The text was set in Catalina Typewriter and Avant Garde Gothic.
Photos by Marianna Balducci and Fabio Gervasoni

Printed in China

www.penguinrandomhouse.ca

1 2 3 4 5   26 25 24 23 22

Penguin
Random House
tundra | TUNDRA BOOKS

TOO
MANY
PIGS

and

ONE
BIG
BAD
WOLF

Davide Cali and Marianna Balducci

tundra

Once upon a time, there were three little pigs.
Then the wolf ate them.
THE END

This story is too short!
I want a longer one!

Once upon a time, there were four little pigs.
The wolf ate the first three.
Then he ate the fourth, but it took longer
because that pig was bigger.
THE END

This story is STILL too short.
There must be other things happening!

Once upon a time, there were five little pigs.
The wolf ate the first, then the second,
then the third, fourth and fifth.
Meanwhile, there was a carnival in the woods.
THE END

The little pigs always get eaten too fast!
And what does a carnival have
to do with anything?

Once upon a time, there were six little pigs.

One was very good at geography.

One was a Sudoku champion.

One slept all the time.

One knew the names of all the stars by heart.

One loved to draw.

One was a skateboarder.

The wolf ate them all.
THE END

What?! Even the skateboarder?

Yes, that one was first.

This story is terrible.

Once upon a time, there were seven little pigs.
One for each color of the rainbow.

And then?

The wolf in yellow ate them all.
THE END

OK, that's enough!
I want a REAL story!

Okay, so once upon a time, there were ten little pigs.

No, eleven.

They formed a soccer team.

The name was Porcellini. No, Dynamo Sausage.

Or was it Olympic Baloney?

Anyway, the wolf ate the goalie last.

THE END

Oh, come on! What was the score?

It was 0 — 0.

UGH! I want a real, whole story,
with a beginning and a middle and an end!

Once upon a time, there were twenty-six little pigs.
Here are their names:
Agamemnon
Babe
Chand
Dennis
Elvis
Fernando
Gerard
Hamilton
Isidore
Jemaine
Kenny
Link
Maxwell
Naheed
Onion
Percival
Quark
Rosita
Sausage
Toot
Ulysses
Vinegar
Wiggly
Xavier
YumYum
Zuimu

The wolf ate them in
alphabetical order.
THE END

Was that a good enough story?

No.

Once upon a time, there were
twenty-nine little pigs.
The wolf ate one a day for a month.
THE END

But aren't there at least thirty days in a month?

It was February. During a leap year.

NOOOOO!

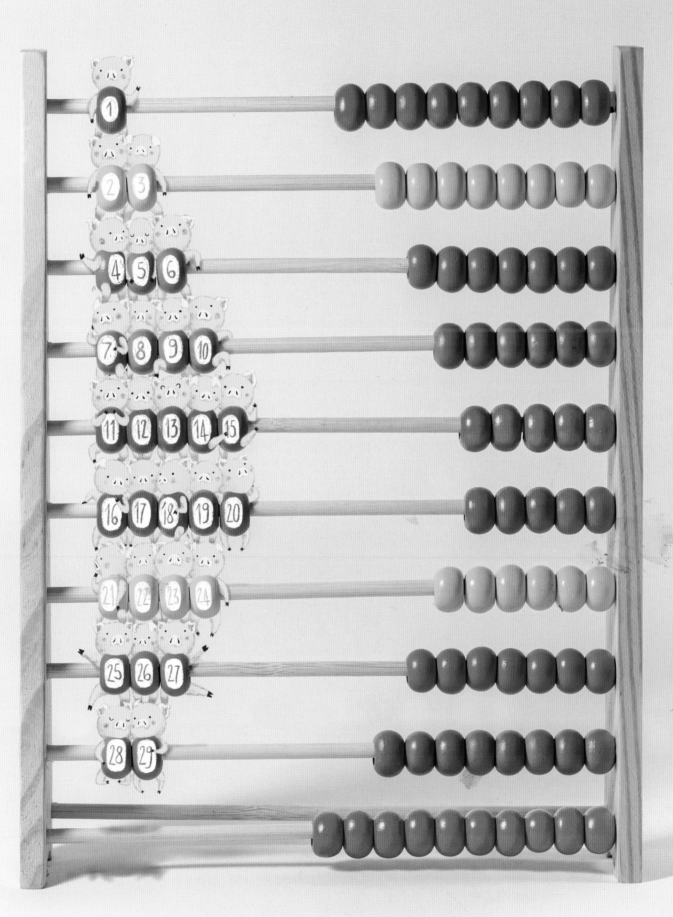

Once upon a time,
there were forty-nine pigs.

Why forty-nine?

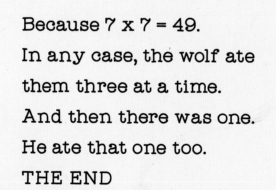

Because 7 x 7 = 49.
In any case, the wolf ate
them three at a time.
And then there was one.
He ate that one too.
THE END

You really can't tell a story that's a little longer?

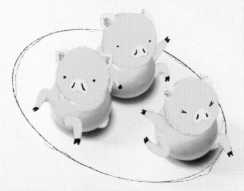

Once upon a time, there were one hundred and one little pigs who wanted to make a movie.

What kind of movie?

An animated film.

What was the title?

It doesn't matter because the wolf ate all one hundred and one little pigs.
THE END

That story was even shorter!!

Once upon a time, there were
three hundred little pigs.

Three hundred? That's a lot!

Yes.

Will it make the story longer?

No, because they were tiny and
the wolf ate them like cereal.
THE END

I can't take this anymore!

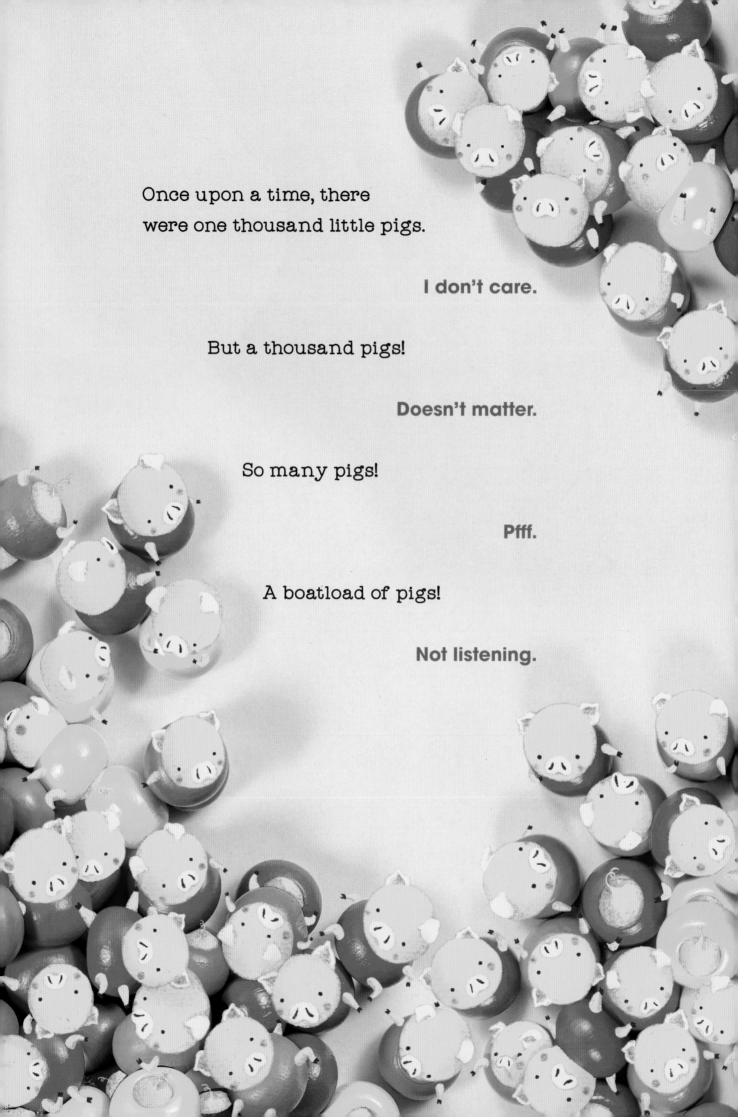

Once upon a time, there
were one thousand little pigs.

I don't care.

But a thousand pigs!

Doesn't matter.

So many pigs!

Pfff.

A boatload of pigs!

Not listening.

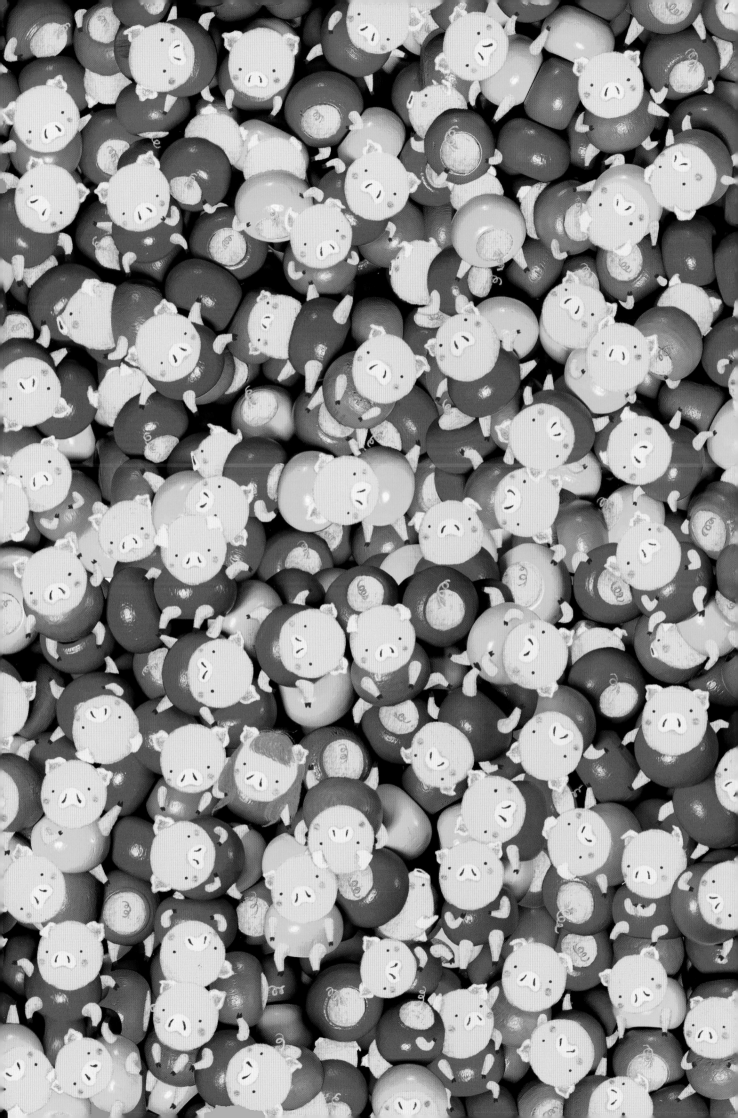

No, he fell asleep because he was full.

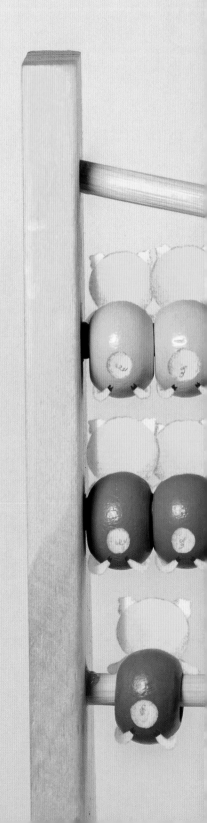